WALT DISNEY PRODUCTIONS
presents

Lady
and the Tramp

Random House 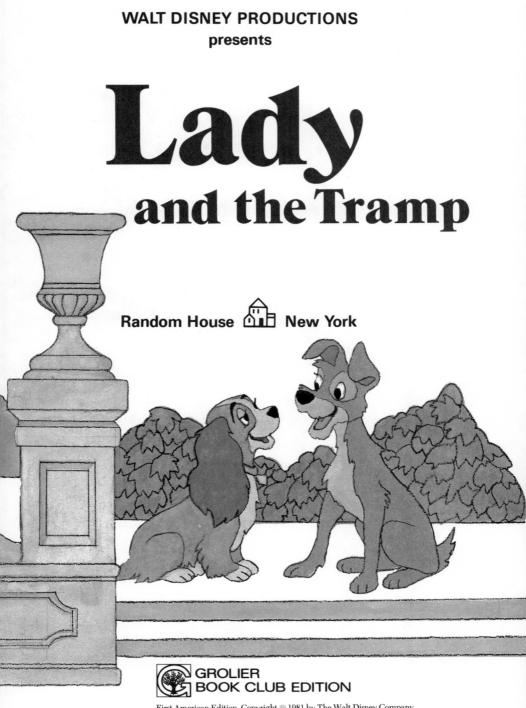 New York

**GROLIER
BOOK CLUB EDITION**

One Christmas Eve Jim Dear
gave his wife Darling a present.
Darling opened the present carefully.
Out popped a little puppy.

"Oh, what a lovely puppy!"
said Darling. "Let's call her Lady."

At bedtime, Jim tucked Lady into a cozy basket.

"That's your very own bed," said Jim.

But Lady didn't want her very own bed.
She was lonely.

So the small puppy climbed
up the big stairs.

She found a much better place to
sleep—right at the foot of Jim's bed.

Every day Lady grew a little bigger.
She did many important things around
the house.

In the morning Lady woke Jim up.

Then Lady brought
Jim his slippers.

Lady barked good morning to the birds
and the butterflies.

She even learned how to pick up the
newspaper and carry it to the house.

Soon Lady made friends with the other
dogs in the neighborhood.

There was a sad-faced bloodhound
called Trusty.

There was a sturdy Scottie called Jock.

Jock showed Lady his
store of hidden bones.

The three of them often
played together.

When Jim came home from work, he whistled.

Lady ran to greet him.

Jim would pat her and say, "Good dog!"

After dinner Lady curled up by the fire.
Darling was knitting tiny clothes.
"It's just the three of us now," said
Darling, "but soon we will have a baby."
Lady was very happy.

One stormy night the doctor came
to the house.
That night the baby was born.

The next morning, Lady
peeked into the bedroom.
"Come in and meet the
new baby," said Darling.
"But don't wake him up!"

Lady looked at the sleeping baby.
"When the baby is bigger you will play together," said Darling.
Lady wagged her tail.
A new baby in the house!

One day Jim told Lady,
"We are going away for a
few days. Aunt Sara is
coming to help. And
you must help too."

"Lady will be a good
babysitter," Darling
said with a smile.

Jim and Darling were in a hurry.

They drove away as soon as Aunt
Sara arrived.

Aunt Sara looked very mean.

Lady hid behind the door.

Then she ran upstairs to guard the baby.

The baby smiled happily
at Lady.

But Aunt Sara was angry.

She swung a broom
at Lady and knocked
over a table.

Lady ran away.

"Get out, you bad dog!" Aunt Sara
yelled. "Get out and stay out!"

Poor Lady!
No one had ever called
her a bad dog before.

She crept away, her ears drooping.

Lady walked and walked.
No one seemed to see her.

But some mean dogs
barked at her.

Lady ran and ran.
At last she ran into
the railroad yard.
Nobody was around.
Finally Lady flopped
down and fell asleep.

Early the next day, a train pulled
into the railroad yard.

Out jumped a big strong dog.

His name was Tramp.

Tramp traveled from place to place.

He took care of himself!

Tramp stretched.

He felt good in this new place.

Then he caught sight of Lady.

At first Lady was afraid.

She remembered the rough looking dogs who had chased her.

But Tramp looked friendly.

Lady liked his face.

"Arf arf!" barked Tramp happily.

He liked Lady right away.

The two walked away together.

Lady trusted Tramp.

FRESH EGGS

Soon they came to a chicken farm.
Tramp's eyes lit up.
He began to dig a hole under
the fence.

Lady watched Tramp.
She looked at the
chickens, too.
She had never seen
chickens before.

Lady followed Tramp under the fence.
SCREECH! CACKLE! SQUAWK!
The chickens were scared.
Lady was scared too!
But Tramp was having a fine time.

What a noise Tramp
and the chickens made!
Suddenly the man from
the dog pound came by.
Tramp ran off.

But Lady wasn't quick
enough.
The man grabbed her
and threw her into
his wagon.

What was Lady to do?
Tramp had disappeared.
She was trapped in a rolling cage.
There were strange dogs all
around her.

But these dogs were friendly.
They liked pretty little Lady.
They told Lady that she would be safe.
She had a dog tag on her collar.

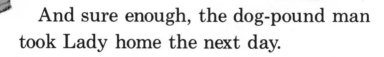

And sure enough, the dog-pound man
took Lady home the next day.

Aunt Sara was not pleased
to see Lady.
She put a big chain on
Lady's collar.

"Stay outside!" she shouted.

Lady couldn't sleep that night.
She heard a rustle in the leaves.

A rat!
It was heading
straight for the
house.

Lady wanted to run after the rat.
But her chain kept her back.

Tramp heard Lady's
bark and came running.
He had been looking for her.
Just then, Lady's chain snapped.

Lady and Tramp ran into the house.
They followed the rat up the stairs.

They found it under the
armchair in the baby's room.

Tramp knew
exactly what
to do with it.

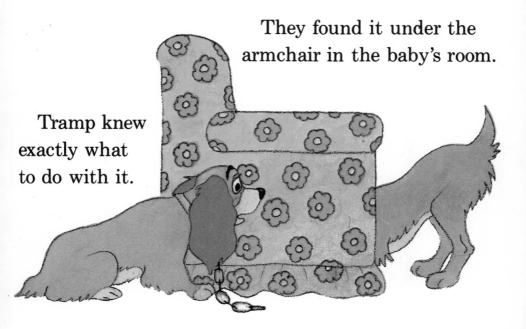

Tramp was tired
after his fight
with the rat.

Suddenly Aunt Sara ran into the room.
She chased Tramp into a closet.
Then she whacked him with a broom.

Just then, Jim and
Darling arrived in
a taxi.

"Thank goodness you are back," said
Aunt Sara. "I found a great big mutt
in the baby's room. And this little
dog wasn't any help!"
And she pointed at Lady.

"What's going on, Lady?" asked Jim.

Lady barked and jumped up and down.

"She's trying to tell us something," said Darling.

Lady ran up the stairs.
Jim followed her.

Lady led him right up to the
big chair where Tramp had
fought with the rat.

Jim saw the dead rat.
He guessed what had
happened.

"That dog helped protect the baby!" he said.

Tramp crept out of the
closet.

"Good brave dog," said Jim.
"You must stay with us forever."

Aunt Sara put on her hat and
walked out.

Tramp became one of the family.
Every day he and Lady went to see the baby.

Tramp made friends with
Trusty and Jock, too.

Soon it was Christmas again.

Jim Dear and Darling were playing
with their baby.

And this Christmas there were some
special presents . . . puppies!

Lady and Tramp were very proud of them!

They all had a happy Christmas together.